The Best of Both Nests

Jane Clarke

Illustrated by **Anne Kennedy**

ALBERT WHITMAN & COMPANY, MORTON GROVE, ILLINOIS

For Julia and Sofia. —J.C.

For John and Jeff. —A.K.

From dawn until dusk every day,
Mr. and Mrs. Stork clattered at each other.

They clattered at each other so loudly that
Stanley had to clatter to be heard.

Sometimes Stanley hid his head under his wing and wished and wished that the clattering would stop.

Then one cloudy Sunday, it did.

"Stanley," Mrs. Stork said, "Dad and I don't sing the same song anymore. All we do is clatter."

"It's making us all unhappy," Dad said. "It's best if I take off. I'm making a new nest across town."

"You'll live here with me during the week," said Mom.

"And with me on the weekends," said Dad. "You'll have two nests, Stanley."

"I don't want two nests!" Stanley said. He clutched his stuffed frog as Dad flew away. "Come back, Dad! You have to be here for Fathers' Flyday on Friday!"

On Monday at school, Stanley's class began to make kites to fly with their fathers on Friday.

"Fathers' Flyday is very special," said Ms. Prance, handing out sticks and string. "I hope everyone's father will come, but you can bring your mother if your father can't make it."

"My daddy can't come," Stella told Stanley. "His nest is way down South. I go there on vacation. Two nests are better than one, we always say."

"Well, I say one nest is best," mumbled Stanley.

On Tuesday, Ms. Prance gave everyone paper and glue for their kites.

"My daddy's nest is lined with pink flamingo feathers," Stella told everyone. "It's great having two nests."

"No, it isn't," muttered Stanley. "One nest is best!"

And for the rest of the day, Stanley glowered at the
sky, and storm clouds glowered back at him.

On Wednesday, Ms. Prance brought out the paint pots.

Stanley slashed swirls and whirls of black and blue paint onto his kite.

"It's a storm, and it's blowing away our nest," Stanley told Ms. Prance.

"Storms are scary," Ms. Prance told him. "But they pass, and the sun always comes out again."

"Always?" asked Stanley.
"Always," said Ms. Prance.

On Wednesday night, Mom made Stanley's favorite worm stew. But his beak quivered.

"It's my fault Dad flew away," Stanley cried. "I wished the clattering would stop, and it did!"

"It's not your fault," Mom said, wrapping him in her wings. "We both love you very much."

That evening, the wind was howling, but it was cozy in the nest, and no one was clattering. Stanley snuggled up while Mom told the story of the stork who delivered the stars to the sky.

On Thursday, Miss Prance's class made tails for their kites.

Stella put butterflies on her kite. Stanley put stars on his.

"There are lots of butterflies where my daddy lives," Stella said.

"My dad likes stars," Stanley told Stella. "I can't wait to show him my kite. It's Flyday tomorrow. It'll be great!"

Stanley brought his kite home to show Mom.

"What lovely stars!" Mom said. "I hope Dad will be there in time to see them tomorrow."

Stanley's feathers drooped.

"He'll have to fly against the wind to get there," Mom explained. "He might miss Fathers' Flyday."

"That's no good!" Stanley wailed, and one by one he pulled the stars off his kite.

The wind blew Stanley to
school early on Flyday Friday.

"My dad's not going to get here on time," Stanley muttered.

"I wish my daddy could be here, too," Stella sighed, "but his nest is too far away."

"It's hard to have two nests," said Stanley.

"Sometimes it is," Stella agreed.

"I guess we have to make the best of it," Stanley told her. "Do you want to help me fix my kite?"

"Okay," said Stella.

"I'll help, too," said Ms. Prance.

And soon Stanley's kite was sprinkled with stars again.

The other fathers arrived, and it was time to fly the
kites. But the wind howled, and the sky was growing
darker and darker. Everyone took off except Stanley
and Stella and Ms. Prance.

"Look at that gap in the clouds," said Ms. Prance.
"Someone's coming down through it."

"It's Dad!" said Stanley. "He made it!"

"Okay, Stanley," Dad said. "It's time
to fly that kite!"
"Can Stella come?" asked Stanley.
"Grab hold of a wing each," said Dad.
"We're taking off!"

The storks swooped and looped across the sky,
pulling their kites. Stanley's stars sparkled, and
Stella's butterflies danced in the sunshine.
They were flying above the storm.

"That was great!" Stanley said when they landed.

Mom was waiting. "Whew!" she said. "The last of the storm has passed."

"It's time to see my new nest," Dad said.

"Can Stella come see it sometime?" Stanley asked.

"Of course," said Dad. "But tomorrow, I'm taking you to a beakball game."

"And I'll have worm stew waiting for you when you get back," said Mom.

Stanley grinned at Stella. "Two nests might
be okay after all," he said.

Mom's Nest

Dad's Nest

Library of Congress Cataloging-in-Publication Data

Clarke, Jane, 1954-
The best of both nests / written by Jane Clarke ; illustrated by Anne Kennedy.
p. cm.
Summary: Stanley the stork is upset when his parents divorce and his father goes to live in a separate nest.
ISBN 13: 978-0-8075-0668-4 (hardcover)
[1. Divorce—Fiction. 2. Storks—Fiction.] I. Kennedy, Anne, 1955- , ill. II. Title.
PZ7.C55355Bes 2007 [E]—dc22 2006023401

Published in 2007 by Albert Whitman & Company, 6340 Oakton Street, Morton Grove, Illinois 60053-2723.
Published simultaneously in Canada by Fitzhenry & Whiteside, Markham, Ontario.

The design is by Carol Gildar.

For more information about Albert Whitman & Company,
visit our web site at www.albertwhitman.com